Curious George®
Mother's Day Surprise

Adaptation by C. A. Krones

**Based on the TV series teleplay
written by Karl Geurs and Raye Lankford**

Houghton Mifflin Harcourt
Boston   New York

For information about permission to reproduce selections from this book, write to trade.permissions@hmhco.com or to Permissions, Houghton Mifflin Harcourt Publishing Company, 3 Park Avenue, 19th Floor, New York, New York 10016.

ISBN: 978-1-328-85716-3 paper over board
ISBN: 978-1-328-89766-4 paperback

Cover art adaptation by Artful Doodlers Ltd.

hmhco.com
curiousgeorge.com

Printed in China
SCP 10 9 8 7 6 5 4 3 2 1
4500689112

AGES	GRADES	GUIDED READING LEVEL	READING RECOVERY LEVEL	LEXILE ® LEVEL
5–7	1	J	17	460L

George loves springtime in the city.
Today, George is playing a concert
in the park with his friend Marco.

The band finished playing and everyone clapped. Then Marco and George heard someone in the crowd say, "What a perfect way to spend Mother's Day!"

"Oh no! We forgot about Mother's Day!" said Marco. "Mami does so much for us. Is it too late to do something special for her today?"

They had
to think fast.
George had an idea.
"Yes, a party!" said Marco.
"Great idea, George."
"We can decorate and cook all of her
favorite foods," said his sister, Cecilia.
"If Mami sees us cooking, she will
want to help," said Marco. "It should
be a surprise!"

"We can have a surprise party at our
house," said the man with the yellow hat.

"Perfect!" said Marco. "Papi can tell
Mami we are on a playdate with George.
Then they can come to pick us up at
five o'clock."

"Great idea," said Cecilia. "But we will have to hurry! Let's get going."

George and Marco rushed home to start
decorating.
"We can make a piñata!" Marco said.
Hundley made a great model.

Cecilia and the man picked out fresh
vegetables at the market: avocados, hot
peppers, carrots, onions, and tomatoes.

At home, everyone helped cook Mami's favorite foods. George prepared the hot peppers . . . very carefully.

Then everyone helped decorate the living room. George hung streamers.

The man helped blow up balloons. The decorating was almost done.

But something was missing.
"We don't have any flowers!" said
Marco. They had to think fast.

Marco had an
idea. "We can
make them out of paper!"
Everyone helped make paper flowers.

15

It took a long time
and made a mess.
Some were better
than others.

By the time they finished the flowers,
it was almost time for the party. Marco
and Cecilia looked outside. "They're
coming! We have to hurry!" said Marco.

Everyone rushed to clean up. They put
the last decorations in place and set the
table with food . . . very quickly.

"They are almost here," said Cecilia.
"Quick, everyone, hide!"

Everyone found a hiding spot just in time.
Some spots were better than others.

When the door opened, they all yelled,
"Surprise!"

"Happy Mother's Day, Mami!" said Marco
and Cecilia. Mami was so surprised.
"This is the best Mother's Day ever!"
she said.

The surprise party was a success! And George and Marco's homemade piñata was a hit, too!

Make Your Own Paper Flowers

Are you having a party like George? Want to give
someone special a gift? Make these flowers!

Here's what you'll need:

- Tissue paper
- Pipe cleaners or ribbon
- Scissors

Step One: Take a stack of 8-12 sheets of
colorful tissue paper that are rectangular
or square shaped.

Step Two: Fold the sheets accordion-style
as if you are making a paper fan.

Step Three: Take a piece of ribbon or a
pipe cleaner and wrap it around the middle
of the long folded stack to keep it together.
Now it looks like a bow.

Step Four: Gently pull each sheet back
toward the pipe cleaner at the center.
Make sure you do this on both sides.

Step Five: Repeat step four on both sides
of the folded stack.

Step Six: Make more flowers and create
a bouquet! Celebrate!